Cora
Cooks
Pancit

Written by
Dorina K. Lazo Gilmore

Illustrated by
Kristi Valiant

 SHEN'S BOOKS

an imprint of Lee & Low Books Inc.

New York

SHEN'S BOOKS, an imprint of LEE & LOW BOOKS INC., 95 Madison Avenue,
New York, NY, 10016, leeandlow.com

Book design by Kristi Valiant
Book production by The Kids at Our House
The text is set in Bell

Manufactured in China by First Choice Printing Co. Ltd.
(HC) 10 9 8 7 6 5 4 3 2 1
(PB) 10 9 8 7 6 5 4
First Edition

Library of Congress Cataloging-in-Publication Data

Lazo Gilmore, Dorina K.
   Cora cooks pancit / by Dorina K. Lazo Gilmore ; illustrated by Kristi Valiant.
      p. cm.
   Summary: When all her older siblings are away, Cora's mother finally lets her
help make pancit, a Filipino noodle dish. Includes recipe for pancit.
   ISBN 978-1-885008-35-0 (HC)   ISBN 978-1-885008-48-0 (PB)
   [1. Cookery, Philippine--Fiction. 2. Filipino Americans--Fiction.] I. Valiant,
Kristi, ill. II. Title.
   PZ7.L4532Co 2009
   [E]—dc22   2008045836

For Rebecca Torosian, who shared her family stories, and in memory of Grandma Cora Taclindo Lazo, who always welcomed me into the kitchen.
-DLG

For my husband, Casey, my favorite blessing, and for my mom, who shares all her recipes with me (except for the secret caramel one).
–KV

Cora loved the kitchen.
She loved to drink in the smells
of Mama's Filipino dishes.

Cora's older sisters and brother often helped with
the cooking. They got the grown-up jobs like shredding
the chicken or mixing noodles in the pot. They sliced
vegetables and rolled *lumpia* into tidy, egg roll shapes.

Cora was stuck with kid jobs like drawing
pictures in the flour or licking spoons.
She longed to be a real cook.

One day Cora's three older sisters headed to the mall. Her brother darted outside with his ball glove. Now was her chance. Cora popped her head around the corner. "What are we making today, Mama?"

Mama wiped her hands on the front of her red apron. She put her hands on her hips: "What would you like to make today?" asked Mama in her buttery voice.

Cora was surprised Mama was letting her decide.
She scrunched up her pug nose and began to think.
All her favorite Filipino foods danced in her head.

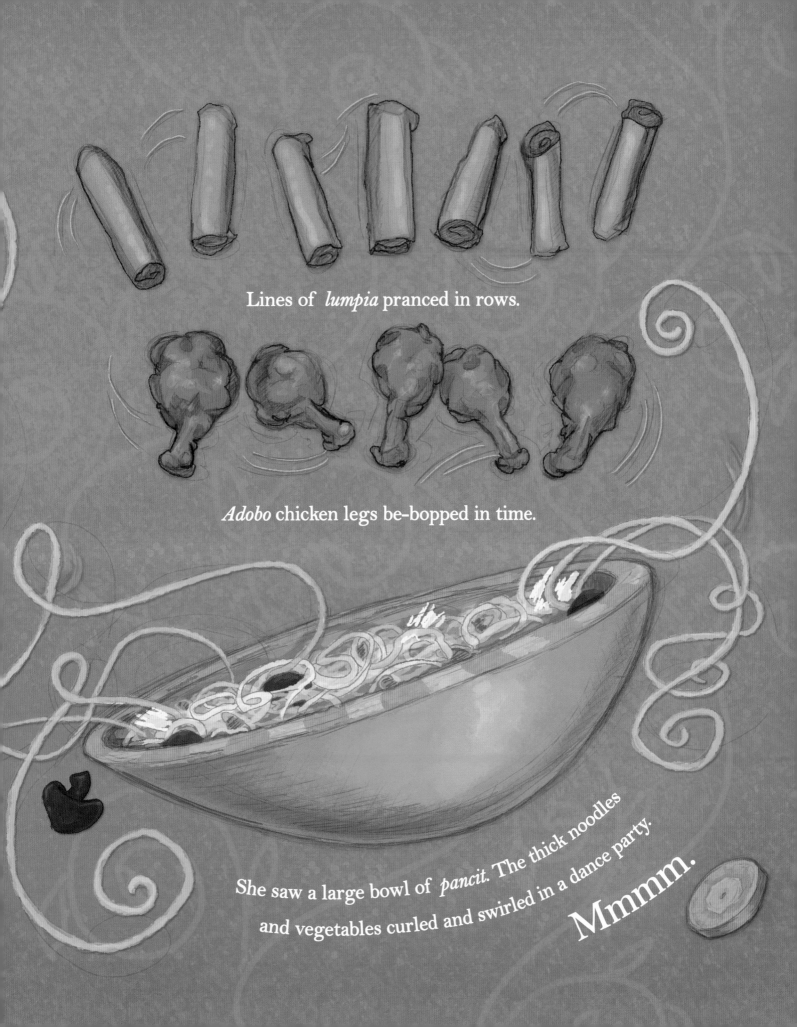

Lines of *lumpia* pranced in rows.

Adobo chicken legs be-bopped in time.

She saw a large bowl of *pancit*. The thick noodles and vegetables curled and swirled in a dance party.

Mmmm.

"Will you teach me to make *pancit*?" she asked.

"Of course," said Mama. "Would you like to wear my red apron?"

Cora was a real cook now. The apron was a little too big, but it would do. Mama helped Cora tie the strings around her back and make a neat bow at her belly button.

"This apron belonged to *Lolo,* your grandpa," said Mama. "He wore it when he first came to California. He was a cook for the Filipino farmworkers who picked strawberries and grapes in the fields."

"Did *Lolo* teach you how to cook?" Cora wanted to know.

"He did," said Mama. "I followed him each day to the big kitchen. He created all kinds of dishes to fill the hungry workers' tummies. While he cooked, he told stories about the Philippines where he was born."

Cora nodded as she listened.

"*Lolo* told us about the countryside where he grew up. His family harvested pineapples, bananas and papayas. He used to eat smashed fried bananas and sweet rice wrapped in banana leaves.

Cora stuffed her hands in the deep apron pockets. She imagined Mama and *Lolo* cooking together. She saw *Lolo* as a boy unwrapping the banana leaves and scooping the sweet rice from inside.

Cora knew the rules in Mama's kitchen.
She scrubbed her hands with soap.

Mama dug in the cupboards and refrigerator for
ingredients. She listed what they needed for the *pancit*.
Chicken. Celery. Carrots. Mushrooms. Onions.
Baby corn. Cabbage. Ginger. Garlic. Soy sauce.

"Don't forget the noodles," said Cora.

"Oh, yes, the noodles," said Mama.

"Let's get started," Mama told Cora. "Open the package of rice noodles and put them in this bowl of water. Do you know why we soak them?"

"So they get soft," answered Cora.

"You've been paying attention," said Mama with a wink. Cora opened the package. She plopped the big clump of noodles into the bowl.

Meanwhile, Mama took out some chicken she had cooked earlier. This was Mama's special stash. She used chicken for all kinds of Filipino dishes like *tanghon*, chicken curry, and *lumpia*.

"Want to help me shred?" asked Mama.

Cora's eyes grew wide. A grown-up job. She was ready. She pulled the chicken pieces apart the way her older sister Prim did. She placed them on a plate. Cora snuck a tiny bite of chicken. She rolled it to the back of her mouth before Mama noticed. The salty taste tickled her tongue.

"I'll chop," said Mama. Cora arranged the vegetables in neat rows. Mama chopped celery stalks, carrots, cabbage and onions. When Mama started slicing onions, tears ran down Cora's cheeks. She looked up and saw Mama's watery eyes.

"Onions make us cry," sang Mama. They both laughed.

Mama took out her huge *pancit* pan with the shiny copper outside and big handles. The pan was deep enough to hold all the ingredients. Cora danced on her tiptoes to see inside. Mama asked Cora to step back while she added some oil and the vegetables to the pan.

The pot began to hiss and sizzle. Mama added spices too – garlic, ginger and a splash of soy sauce.

Mmmm. Cora loved the smell of garlic.

"Can you check the noodles, Cora?" asked Mama.

Cora scratched her head. She tried to remember what her sister Sara did when she checked the noodles. Cora thought she should sniff the noodles, but she picked up the bowl too quickly. Water sloshed onto the floor.

"Are you making a mess?" asked Mama with pointy eyebrows. "Silly, Cora. You just need to touch the noodles with two fingers to see if they are soft."

Mama laughed and handed Cora a towel to mop up the mess. Mama went to work straining the noodles.

"Now for the fun part," said Mama. "Let's add the noodles to the pancit pan."

"Can I stir?" asked Cora. She knew this was another grown-up job.

"Yes, but be careful near the burner," called Mama, who pulled out a stool for Cora to stand on. Cora began to stir in a wide circle. She watched the noodles somersault over the carrots and celery. She made the soft onions sway this way and that. The smell of ginger mixing with garlic floated to her nose.

A few mushrooms escaped from the pot.

Oops.

That night, Mama brought the food to the table. She set out a platter of *adobo* chicken, two plates of her special *lumpia* with dipping sauce, and a bowl of pineapple slices. Cora's brother and sisters came to the table one by one. Daddy sat in his usual spot at the head of the table. Cora watched his eyes grow wide as he checked out all the food. He licked his lips.

Finally, Mama set the steaming platter of *pancit* in the middle of the table.

"You made *pancit* without us!" hollered Cora's brother Crispin.

"Who did my job?" asked Prim.

"Who checked the noodles?" Sara needed to know.

Mama replied, "Cora did all the grown-up jobs."

"Really?" said Daddy. "That's my girl!"

Cora scrunched together her eyebrows and bit her lip
while the family tasted her *pancit*.

Did she do everything right? Would they like it?
Would Mama tell about the accident with the noodles?

"Pretty impressive," smiled Cora's sister Irene.

Crispin chomped on a big spoonful of *pancit* and elbowed Cora. "Not too bad," Crispin said.

Cora grinned. Her eyes sparkled with delight.

Daddy sat back in his chair. "This tastes like your *Lolo's* pancit," he said.

Cora beamed with pride. "*Salamat,*"
she cried out. "Thank you!"
The family laughed. Cora was still
wearing Mama's red apron.

GLOSSARY

In the Philippines, more than 200 dialects and languages are spoken in different parts of the islands. Tagalog is one of the more common languages. Some words sound similar to Spanish. Check out the meanings of these words found in the story.

Adobo (ah-DOH-bo) is a way of cooking meat using vinegar and soy sauce. There are different versions of adobo chicken and pork.

Lolo (LO-lo) means "grandpa."

Lumpia (LOOM-pee-ah) is the Filipino version of egg rolls often filled with vegetables and sometimes meat and then wrapped and fried.

Pancit (pan-SEET) is a popular noodle dish prepared in a variety of ways, depending on the family and region they are from. The noodles are combined with vegetables and spices and sometimes meat. The pancit noodles are called "rice stick" noodles.

Salamat (sah-LA-mat) means "Thank you."

Tanghon (tang-HONE) is a made with a clear noodle called vermicelli. The noodles are combined with vegetables and often served as a side dish.

LOLO'S PANCIT RECIPE

1½ pounds boned chicken plus 1 cup water and 1 teaspoon soy sauce
or 3 boneless chicken breasts plus ½ cup chicken broth and 1 teaspoon soy sauce

1 (8-ounce) package rice stick pancit noodles

1 (8-ounce) package dried shiitake mushrooms

1 yellow onion, chopped

2 tablespoons plus ¼ cup soy sauce

2 garlic cloves, finely chopped

1 tablespoon fresh ginger, finely chopped

1 tablespoon vegetable or olive oil

½ head cabbage, shredded

2 carrots, thinly sliced

3 celery stalks, sliced

1 (8-ounce) can water chestnuts, sliced

1 (8-ounce) can bamboo shoots, sliced

1 (8-ounce) can baby corn, diced

1½ cups water or chicken broth

3 eggs, hard-boiled and sliced

5 green onions, sliced lengthwise and cut into 3-inch strips (optional)

salt and pepper

Chicken can be prepared ahead of time. Steam boned chicken in a large pot with water and 1 teaspoon soy sauce for 25 minutes. (Easy alternative: Cook boneless chicken breasts, chicken broth, and 1 teaspoon soy sauce in a crock pot or slow cooker on high for 3 hours or on low for 6 hours.) Cool chicken and shred.

Soak noodles in warm water for approximately 30 minutes. Soak mushrooms in a separate bowl of warm water for 30 minutes. Meanwhile, cut up vegetables.

Strain mushrooms. Heat chicken, mushrooms, yellow onion, and 2 tablespoons soy sauce in a non-stick skillet. Stir in garlic and ginger. Sprinkle with salt and pepper. Set aside.

Heat 1 tablespoon oil in a large, shallow pot. Add cabbage, carrots, celery, water chestnuts, bamboo shoots, and baby corn. Sprinkle with salt and pepper. Cook briefly, keeping the cabbage and carrots a little crisp. Add chicken and mushroom mixture.

Strain noodles. Add to pot with chicken, all vegetables, and 1½ cups water or chicken broth. Stir together. Add ¼ cup soy sauce. Cook for 10 to 15 minutes until noodles and vegetables are soft and combined.

Garnish with sliced hard-boiled eggs and green onions, if using. The green onions will begin to curl when cut this way. Serve.

Makes 10-12 (2-cup) servings.

Note: Children should make pancit with the help of an adult.
Preparation involves chopping, cutting, and sautéing on the stove.